ICE AGE™

CONTINENTAL DRIFT

THE JUNIOR NOVEL

HarperFestival is an imprint of HarperCollins Publishers.

Ice Age™: Continental Drift: The Junior Novel
Ice Age: Continental Drift™ and © 2012 Twentieth Century Fox Film Corporation.
All Rights Reserved. Printed in the United States of America.
No part of this book may be used or reproduced in any manner whatsoever
without written permission except in the case of brief quotations embodied in critical articles
and reviews. For information address HarperCollins Children's Books,
a division of HarperCollins Publishers, 10 East 53rd Street, New York, NY 10022.
www.harpercollinschildrens.com
www.iceagemovie.com
Library of Congress catalog card number: 2012934236
ISBN 978-0-06-210485-4
12 13 14 15 16   LP/BR   10 9 8 7 6 5 4 3 2 1
❖
First Edition

ICE AGE™
CONTINENTAL DRIFT

THE JUNIOR NOVEL

ADAPTED BY
SUSAN KORMAN

HARPER FESTIVAL
An Imprint of HarperCollinsPublishers

ICE AGE™
CONTINENTAL DRIFT

THE JUNIOR NOVEL

"**W**hoa!" Manny cried. The woolly mammoth's eyes snapped open one morning as a loud, rumbling noise shook the valley around him. "What was that?" He whirled toward his mate, Ellie. "Did you hear that sound?"

"I heard it, Manny," Ellie said. "But whatever it is, it's miles away."

"Peaches?" Manny's eyes darted nervously to the tree branch where his teenage daughter slept. "Are you alright?"

The branch was empty, sending Manny into a fresh panic. "Where is she?" he cried. "It's early! No teenager ever wakes up this early!"

"Easy, warden," Ellie teased him. "This isn't prison. Peaches is not on lockdown, remember?"

But Manny was already in action, moving toward another branch, the one where the possums, Crash and Eddie, slept.

Whack! Manny hit the tree hard with his trunk, instantly waking up the two brothers.

"You two are supposed to be responsible uncles!" Manny yelled. "Why weren't you watching Peaches?"

"Huh? What?" Crash blinked as he shook himself awake. "I didn't see a thing," he said. "Really, Manny. I didn't see Peaches sneak off fifteen or twenty minutes ago."

"Me either," Eddie chimed in. "I didn't see her sneak off with Louis and head to the Falls either."

"The Falls!" Manny shrieked. "She went to the Falls? That's where all the delinquents go!"

"Relax, Manny," Ellie said calmly. "It's just where kids hang out."

"Oh no, it isn't!" Manny shot back. "It's a gateway hangout that leads right to trouble! First, it's hanging out at the Falls, and then, it's piercing her trunk. The next thing you know, Peaches will be addicted to berries!"

"Manny," Ellie said. She couldn't help laughing at him. "You're overreacting. Peaches is not going to be your little girl forever."

"I know that," Manny informed his mate. "And that's exactly what worries me!"

"Whoa! This is fun!" In another part of the valley, Peaches was grinning as she swung from tree branch to tree branch. Looking down, she could see her best friend burrowing along in the ground directly below her.

"Hey, Louis!" Peaches said, teasing the molehog. "Would you get your head out of the ground for once and try to have a little fun?"

Louis popped up suddenly, bumping his head on a tree root. "Ow," he muttered. Then he looked up at Peaches. "I'm a mole-hog," he reminded her. "And my idea of fun isn't risking death so that you can meet some cute mammoth."

"Ethan isn't *cute*," Peaches corrected Louis. "He's hot! Besides," she went on, "You can't spend your whole life playing it safe."

"I know I would," a voice suddenly boomed.

"Dad!" Peaches cried. Manny stood in front of her, a furious look on his face. "There's no reason to be mad!" Peaches said quickly.

Manny continued glaring at her. "You know how I feel about you going to the Falls, Peaches," he said. "Especially alone."

"She's not alone, sir," Louis piped up.

"You don't count," Manny snapped at

the rodent. Then he turned back to Peaches. "Come on, young lady. We're going home where I can keep an eye on you."

With a sigh, Peaches turned around and began to follow her father back home. Louis stared uncertainly after them for a second. "Sir?" he finally called to Manny. "Should I just stay here, or—"

A loud rumble interrupted him. Terrified, Louis ducked back into the ground and began burrowing deep into the earth.

Diego the saber-toothed tiger leaped across some boulders and stared down over the valley. A loud rumble, growing even louder by the second, echoed all around him. The saber-toothed tiger lifted his head and roared back.

"You don't scare me, Mother Nature!" he declared boldly. "There's nothing you can throw at me that I can't handle!"

Crash! Just then a sled loaded with sloths burst through some nearby bushes. Before Diego could get out of its path, the sled slammed into him. Diego gripped the front of the sled, desperately trying to hang on as it carried him along.

"I think we're almost there," the mother sloth, Eunice, was saying to the rest of the family.

"We'd better be almost there," the father, Milton, retorted. "I just lost the sled's steering!"

A grandmother sloth was tied to the top of the sled. "Has anyone seen Precious?" she called out. "It's her feeding time."

"Mom!" Marshall, the boy sloth, whined. "Granny is talking about her dead pet again!"

The sled was streaking toward a sickening drop.

"Paws up, everybody!" the sloth named Uncle Fungus yelled, raising his arms and pretending he was on a roller coaster.

"Ew!" Marshall cried as he sniffed Fungus's armpits. "Paws down, Uncle, please! That is nasty!"

The sled suddenly went airborne. "Be careful, Milton!" Eunice called out. "The sled is going to hurt somebody. . . . Ahhh!"

Wham! Eunice let out a startled scream as she saw what they hit. Diego was still clinging to the front of the sled. But now he was frantically trying to climb aboard before the sled crashed into something else.

Boom!

The sled hit a tall rock. Diego was thrown to the back of the sled, and so was Granny, both of them tangled in vines. As the sled started moving again, the other sloths leaned hard to the side, trying to keep it from tipping over.

Just then, Diego spotted Manny marching Peaches toward home. Ellie stood there, waiting for the two of them.

"So tell me, Dad," Peaches was asking in frustration. "When exactly will I be allowed to hang out with boys?"

"When I'm dead," Manny informed her. "Plus three days, just to make sure that I'm dead."

Oh no, thought Diego. *The sled is headed right at Peaches!* Springing into action, Diego flung himself at a nearby tree and gripped its trunk tightly. The vine entangling him pulled taut, instantly stopping the sled. As it halted—just inches from Peaches—the family of sloths flew off, slamming into Manny and knocking him down.

"Manny!" Ellie cried, racing over. "Are you okay?"

Manny climbed to his feet, brushing off sloths. "Get off my face," he snapped at them. Diego was just as annoyed at the sloth family. He stuck his face into Uncle Fungus's face. "That was fun," the saber-toothed tiger said sarcastically. "Now which one of you should I eat first?"

"Uncle Fungus?" a familiar voice called. "Could that really be you?"

Manny looked up as someone pushed his way through the small crowd gathered around the sloths.

"Excuse me . . . sorry . . ." It was Sid. "Mom! Dad! Marshall!" he cried.

Manny blinked in surprise. Sid knew these sloths?

"Granny's here, too!" Sid cried in excitement. "Wow! My whole family is here!"

Manny and his family watched in amazement as Sid gathered the other sloths into a big hug. "See," Manny said, nudging Peaches. "Sid still hugs *his* parents."

Eunice was gazing lovingly at Sid. "I never thought I'd see my little baby again," she gushed. "We've been searching everywhere for you!"

"You have?" said Sid, beaming. "I knew it! Deep down I knew I wasn't abandoned."

The other sloths stepped out of his hug.

"That's incorrect," his brother, Marshall, said. "We totally abandoned you."

"Then, for a couple of years," Milton chimed in, "we actively avoided you."

"But we always missed you," Eunice added, elbowing her mate hard. "Isn't that right, Milton?"

"Oh yes!" said Milton. "And we just knew Sid would want to see his poor dear granny before . . . um . . . well, before her time is up."

"I'll bury you all and dance on your graves!" Granny snapped.

"See, Sid?" Eunice chimed in. "Granny can't wait to spend time with you."

They all looked over at Granny. While Marshall was busy using a piece of ice as a magnifying glass to burn ants, Granny was busy using a piece of ice to burn Marshall's ear.

"Ow!" Marshall cried, making Granny laugh gleefully.

Milton brought Granny over to Sid. "Why don't you show her your cave?" he suggested. "She could use a nap."

"Sure!" Sid said. He began leading his grandmother away. "I've got so much to tell you, Granny," he said. "A lot has happened since the last time I saw you."

Granny shook her head. "I'm not interested," she told Sid.

As soon as Sid and Granny were out of

earshot, the other sloths cheered.

"Yahoo!" Milton cried. "We got rid of the crazy old bat. Let's go! Move, everybody!"

Sid's friends watched in disbelief as the four sloths jumped back onto the sled.

"Wait!" cried Manny. "You can't just leave. Sid will be crushed."

"Sorry, cookie," Eunice replied. "Things are breaking apart back home."

"So we're heading inland," Milton added. "And Granny is just dead weight."

"See you!" Eunice added brightly. They waved good-bye and then the sloths took off again. But before they disappeared from view, Milton glanced back over his shoulder one more time. "You'd better warn the community," he called. "Granny tends to stray!"

3

Manny stood there with Diego and Ellie, staring after the sloths' sled.

"Well, that explains a lot about Sid," murmured Diego.

A moment later Sid was back with Granny. "Mom! Dad!" he called. "Do you have Granny's teeth? She can't find them anywhere."

Toothless, Granny was trying to chew some fruit. Finally, she took the food out of her mouth and shoved it at Sid. "Hey! Can you chew this thing for me?"

Sid backed away in disgust. "Guys?" he said, looking around for his family again. "Hello?" Suddenly, he glanced uncertainly at his friends. "Where is everyone?" he asked.

Manny and Ellie looked at each other. Neither one of them wanted to tell Sid the upsetting truth.

"I'll handle this," Diego said bravely. "Sid, I'm sorry," he said, looking directly into Sid's eyes. "But your family was wiped out by an asteroid."

"What?" Sid blinked in confusion.

Manny jumped in. "What Diego is trying to say, Sid, is that your family left. They only wanted to find you so you could take care of Granny," he explained.

"Oh, come on!" Sid scoffed. "What kind of sick family would come and ditch their old granny on someone? That's just . . ." His words trailed off for a second as he thought about it. "*My* kind of sick family would do that," he added with a sigh.

"At least you still have Granny, right, buddy?" Diego put in gently.

Sid looked over at his grandmother. But to his surprise, she was gone. "Granny!" he called. "Where are you?"

"Wow," Ellie said. "For an old girl, Granny moves fast." Soon everyone had joined in the search. "Granny! Where are you?"

"Come out, come out, wherever you are," Sid called.

The only reply was another distant rumble from the ground.

At last, Sid tried something new. "Here, Granny. I have prunes for you." He spat some chewed prunes into his hand and held them out, hoping to tempt her. "And they're prepared just the way you like them!"

Manny looked away in disgust. "I don't want to see that," he muttered. Manny scanned the landscape one more time. Suddenly, he gasped. "Oh no!"

Everyone looked over anxiously, expecting

to see that something terrible had happened to poor Granny. But something else had caught Manny's eye. It was Peaches and Louis—sneaking back to the Falls!

As they walked along, Louis was trying to persuade Peaches to turn around. "What if your dad finds out?" he asked her. "Have you fully considered this, Peaches?"

"Wait! Shh!" Peaches shushed Louis so she could listen to something. "Do you hear that?"

The two of them peered down below an overlook. Steep ridges surrounded tar pools and clusters of sharp rocks. A bunch of teenagers were hanging out near a frozen waterfall, playing and listening to music.

Peaches scanned the crowd and quickly located a mammoth with stylish hair. "Hey, look, Louis," she said excitedly. "There's Ethan!"

Louis had spotted Ethan, too. The mammoth was standing near a group of girls, and they were all watching an elk slide down the frozen waterfall.

"Wow. . . ," everyone murmured as the elk launched himself high into the air.

"See," Peaches said to Louis. "It's fun here, not dangerous."

Just then a geyser shot up from a tar pool, hitting the elk and knocking him out of the air. Everyone gasped as he crashed to the ground.

Louis shot Peaches a look.

"I'm sure he's fine," Peaches told Louis quickly.

Ethan was grinning and shaking his head in amazement as the elk got up and wobbled around. "You did not just do that! That was crazy!" Ethan exclaimed, giving him a high five.

"Isn't Ethan perfect?" Peaches asked with a dreamy sigh.

"'Perfect' is a strong word," Louis muttered. "How about 'adequate'?"

Crash and Eddie were hiding in some nearby bushes. Eddie was confused. "Who are we stalking?" he asked. "Is it Ethan?"

Crash answered, "I bet it's Ethan." He

caught sight of Louis and greeted him. "Oh hey, Louis."

"Hey!" Peaches cried. "What are you two doing here?" she demanded.

"Manny told us to keep an eye on you," Eddie explained.

"But not to let you see us," Crash said.

"Under any circumstances," Eddie added.

The two possums looked at each other, realizing they had blown their cover. "Stupid! Stupid! Stupid!" they cried, smacking each other.

Ignoring the possums, Peaches turned back to the Falls. She took a deep breath to calm herself. "Okay," she said. "I'm going for it. Do I look okay, Louis?"

Louis glanced at her adoringly. "'Okay' doesn't even begin to cover it."

Peaches beamed at the molehog. "Oh, Louis, you're the greatest friend ever!"

Louis forced himself to smile. "That's me! A great friend!"

Peaches started toward the ridge, muttering to herself as she rehearsed what she was going to say to Ethan. "Hi, Ethan! My name is Peaches. What's yours?" Then she shook her head, disgusted with the way she sounded. "Ugh! What am I doing? Okay," she told herself. "Just be cool. Just be—*aagh!*"

Peaches let out a scream as she suddenly tumbled over the ridge. She landed hard on the slippery waterfall slide. "Ow! Ow! Ow!" she cried, bumping her way down the frozen surface.

The group of teenagers looked up and stared at Peaches flying backward down the slide. Then a few let out a loud cheer. They thought she was doing some kind of crazy stunt!

"Yo," Ethan murmured. "That's intense."

"Ow, ow, ow!" Peaches kept yelling. "This hurts so much!" A second later she sailed off the slide, heading right at the tar geysers.

"No, no, no!" Peaches cried, frantically cartwheeling through the geysers. A second later she finally landed—right on top of Ethan!

Whoa . . . ," Ethan murmured. Stunned, he shook his head and blinked at Peaches. "What just happened?"

"Gross," one of the teenage mammoth girls said loudly when she saw Peaches. "It's that weirdo who chills with possums."

Peaches tried to get up. "Oh no . . . ," she said, realizing that her tusks were locked with Ethan's. "Oh, Ethan, I am so sorry. . . . Wow!" She blushed as she gazed into the handsome mammoth's eyes. "You're even better looking up close!" she blurted out. "You're phenomenal! I mean—"

Ethan stared at her in a daze, his vision still blurred. "Why do I see two of you?" he mumbled.

"Am I interrupting something?" an angry voice growled.

Oh no. Peaches's heart sank as her father approached. "Dad!" Quickly, she tried again to free her tusks from Ethan's.

Once Manny stood in front of them, Ethan's vision seemed to clear instantly. "Oh boy," he said with a gulp. "Okay . . . uh . . . I . . . um . . ."

Manny yanked on Peaches to pull her away, but her tusks were still interlocked with Ethan's.

"Sorry." Peaches flushed and apologized

again to Ethan. She stared at the tusks for a second, trying to figure out how they could pull them apart. "If I just move left . . . ," she murmured. "No, you go left."

"Just move back a bit," Ethan suggested. "That should do it. No . . . that way."

Manny finally reached in to pull the two of them apart. Then he got right in Ethan's face. "You!" he snarled. "Keep away from my daughter."

"Dad," Peaches began. "Trust me. Nothing—"

"And you!" Manny cut her off with a snarl. "You're grounded!"

"But I didn't do—"

"Grounded!" Manny repeated.

The teen mammoths who'd been hanging out with Ethan snickered loudly.

"Ouch," said the one named Katie. "That's her dad."

"Seriously, that's embarrassing!" said Steffie.

"What a freak!" chimed in their friend Meghan.

"I hear her mom was raised by possums," said Steffie.

Fuming, Peaches stomped away from Manny. She'd never forgive him for this.

"Peaches!" Manny hurried after her. "Come on! Let's talk about this!"

Finally, she whirled around. "How could you embarrass me in front of my friends!" she demanded.

"You deliberately went where you weren't supposed to!" Manny yelled back.

"You can't control my life!"

"I'm trying to protect you! That's what fathers do!"

"Well, I wish you weren't my father!" Peaches shouted.

Manny froze, stung by his daughter's words. Ellie came toward them.

"She's just upset, honey," Ellie told Manny. Then she turned to her daughter. "Peaches, what happened is not the end of the world."

Before Peaches could argue back, there was a loud rumble all around them.

"Ooh!" Sid said, rubbing his stomach. "Excuse me!"

"I don't think that was your stomach, Sid," Diego said, looking about with alarm.

The ground trembled and then a thin crack snaked its way along the ice, cutting right between Manny and his family.

"Uh . . ." Ellie stared down at the crack, and then looked back up at Manny. "What's that?" she asked nervously. An ominous rumble answered her question; this one was louder than the previous sounds.

"I don't know," Manny said. "But stay right there. I'll come to you." He stepped toward his family.

Boom! All at once the crack exploded open, sending everyone flying. Then the deafening sound of rocks shearing apart filled the air.

"Ellie!" Manny reached forward with his trunk, linking hers to his. But the ice shelf under his feet had broken off from the rest of the continent and was already starting to drift away.

"Manny!" Ellie screamed as the mammoths'

trunks were rapidly pulled apart. "No!"

Sid and Diego scrambled up behind Manny. The ice shelf was sliding toward the open glacial bay.

Manny raced along the iceberg in a panic.

"Hurry, Dad!" yelled Peaches. "Hurry!"

Manny looked down. Below was a steep drop to the water. But he had to get to Ellie and Peaches. He tensed, ready to leap across the water toward his family.

"Manny!" Diego yelled, suddenly slamming into him and knocking him down.

"Diego?" Manny looked up at his friend, stunned. "Why'd you do that?"

"You never would have made it!" Diego said breathlessly.

Manny looked down at the water. Diego was right. By now it was a huge abyss. Chunks of ice as large as trucks were crashing into the water around them.

All around Ellie and Peaches, the land was crumbling fast. Then a menacing wall of rock rose up behind them.

Manny stared at it in horror. "Ellie!" he

shouted. "Look behind you!" Frantic, he glanced around and spotted a land bridge. "Go to the land bridge!" he shouted at her. "The land there looks stable. You'll be safe on the other side!"

But Ellie didn't want to leave him. "No, Manny, no!" she protested.

Manny's eyes were fixed now on the moving tower of rock. "You have to get out of there! Go! Now!" he screamed.

The two mammoths stared at each other, filled with terror as the distance between them rapidly widened. They both knew that Manny was right—Ellie and Peaches had to go at once. They also knew that their family was about to be separated, maybe even forever.

By now, a strong current had caught Manny's iceberg and was carrying it out toward the open sea.

"Mom!" cried Peaches, stepping toward the edge of land.

"No, Peaches," Ellie yelled at her daughter. "Get back!"

Boom! A huge mountain behind them

shuddered and then tumbled down. Rocks cascaded everywhere.

"Daddy!" Peaches cried.

"Stay alive!" Manny called back helplessly. His family was in terrible danger, but there was nothing he could do to help them.

At last, Peaches and Ellie turned around and began running away.

"I'll find you!" Manny yelled after them. "No matter how long it takes, I will find you!"

As Manny's iceberg disappeared from view, Peaches clutched Ellie and sobbed. "This is all my fault!" she wailed. "If only I had listened to Dad and stayed away from the Falls!"

"Peaches!" Ellie said sharply. "This is

not your fault. Okay?"

"But . . ." Peaches sobbed. "What if I never see him again? The last thing we did was fight!"

"Your father is the toughest, most stubborn mammoth I've ever met," Ellie told her firmly. "He'll come back for us. That's a promise."

Peaches nodded, finally calming down a little. As Ellie hugged her daughter, she was glad that Peaches couldn't see the worry deep in Ellie's eyes.

Out on the open sea Manny looked around their iceberg—there was a cluster of trees and some rocks, but not much else. Desperate to turn the iceberg around, he found a log and started using it like an oar. "Come on!" he yelled to Sid and Diego. "Help me turn this thing around!"

Diego and Sid knew it was hopeless, but they started paddling, too.

"They need me," Manny went on. "We've got to get back!"

"Buddy," Diego told him gently. "This iceberg is too big to turn. And the current is pulling us out pretty quickly."

Manny just kept paddling.

"You know," Sid said to Manny a few minutes later, "my mother once told me that bad news is just good news in disguise."

"Was this before she abandoned you?" Diego wanted to know.

"Yes, it was," admitted Sid. "But the point is, even though things look bad, there's a rainbow around every corner." By now, the wind was blowing harder, and a huge swell had lifted the iceberg. But Sid didn't notice a thing as he kept paddling. "And there's nothing but smooth sailing ahead!" he went on brightly.

"Smooth sailing ahead, huh, Sid?" Manny echoed, looking up at the dark storm clouds overhead and the ocean water churning around them.

Thundering noises filled the valley as the land continued shifting. "Settle down, everyone," Ellie called to the animals who were lined up, ready to evacuate. "Stay calm. Don't panic."

But Peaches, like everyone else, was already panicking. "Wait, Mom!" she cried. "Where's Louis? We have to find him."

Ellie hesitated, anxiously eyeing the wall of rock again that was pushing toward them. They were running out of time—it was coming closer every second. "Okay," she said finally. "You can look for him. But you have to make it fast, Peaches."

"Got it!" Peaches assured her mother. Then she started shouting, "Louis! Where are you? Come on, we have to go!"

Ellie joined the search, along with Crash and Eddie.

"Louis!" they all yelled again and again.

At last, Peaches heard a scrambling sound. "Louis!" she cried, spotting him running along the ridge that overlooked the Falls. Suddenly, the land under his feet began to give way.

"Peaches!" Louis cried. "Help!"

"You have to jump!" she yelled at him.

"Go!" he called back. "Save yourself!"

"We're not leaving without you," Peaches cried.

"Thank goodness," Louis said in relief.

Peaches raced along below him. "Jump!" she yelled again.

Louis leaped off the ridge as the land all around him—the entire cliff along with the frozen waterfall—collapsed. He landed on Peaches's back and then scrambled down her shoulders. He hung from her trunk, his eyes closed in exhaustion.

"Thanks for coming back for me," he said.

"What do you mean?" Peaches replied. "You don't leave a friend behind."

"Let's go," Ellie told them urgently. "The wall is going to continue moving toward the coast, and we have to make it to the land bridge before it's too late."

She started moving, and so did the other animals. But Peaches and Louis hung back for one more second, gazing at the land- scape. They couldn't believe it. The Falls, where they had just been hanging out earlier that day, was completely destroyed.

"Keep your eye on the horizon!" Manny shouted to Diego and Sid. As the violent storm surged, huge waves crashed over their iceberg.

"I can't find the horizon!" Diego yelled back. Below them, the sea rolled violently. The three animals clung tightly to the iceberg, desperately trying to hang on.

Sid's eyes suddenly filled with terror. A massive tidal wave loomed in front of them! The three friends screamed as they sailed up the enormous wall of water and then plummeted back down into the ocean.

"Ha-ha!" Sid laughed in glee. "We made it. Come on, ocean! Is that the best you can do?"

A giant waterspout shot up, as if it were answering his question. The swirling spout pulled in their iceberg and lifted them skyward again, this time high above the dark clouds.

"Hey!" Sid cried. In the distance he could see clear skies—and a rainbow. "I told you, Manny! My mother was right. There *is* a rainbow around every corner!"

Before Manny could answer, they slammed back down in the water, landing with a loud *splash*!

"Peaches!" Louis shouted in warning. "Watch out!"

Peaches was so lost in her thoughts, she didn't see the enormous landslide that was thundering toward them like a high-speed train. It came right at her, carrying rocks, trees, and other debris with it.

Louis pushed her out of the way in the nick of time.

"Are you okay?" Louis asked her. "You didn't even hear that landslide approaching!"

Peaches nodded, miserable. "I'm just so worried about my dad."

"We're going to get to him," Louis reassured her. "At this pace we'll stay ahead of the rock wall, and we'll make it to the land bridge before you know it. We're all going to survive this," he went on.

Just then, Crash and Eddie fell into a huge trench that had been carved out by the landslide.

"Well," added Louis, looking at the possums. "Maybe those two won't survive this. But everyone else will be totally fine."

Peaches nodded, desperately wanting to believe her friend's words.

6

Manny shook himself off, spraying water everywhere. He was soaking wet—and stranded in the middle of an endless ocean.

"Our iceberg is still heading away from home," he told his friends grimly.

"Yeah," Sid agreed. "But we survived," he pointed out. "And we still have each other. Things could be worse, right?"

"For once he's actually right, Manny," Diego said. "We made it through storms and tidal waves. What more can they hit us with?"

Just then something clobbered him on the head with a stick.

"Ow!" cried Diego, startled.

He whipped around to see a long stick protruding from a hollow tree stump on the iceberg. He peered inside the tree stump and heard someone muttering, "Don't make me get up if I don't want to get up. If I want to get up, I'll get up! Right now, I don't want to."

"Hello?" called Diego. This time the stick, which was actually someone's cane, jabbed him sharply in the eye.

"Ouch!" Diego cried.

"I'm trying to sleep," a familiar voice snapped.

"Granny?" Sid cried. "You're alive!"

"And can we say how thrilled we are to see

you," muttered Diego sarcastically.

"Hey, Fats," Granny called to Manny. "Want to get me out of here?"

Manny tried to use his trunk to yank the old sloth out of the stump, but she was wedged in too tightly.

"Come on!" Granny said, irritated. "Why don't you pretend I'm dessert? That should motivate you!"

Manny pulled again. At last, the old sloth flew out of the tree stump with a loud *pop*!

Manny stared at her. "I can't believe you were in that tree stump the whole time. You slept through that storm?" he asked.

"I slept through the comet that killed the unicorns," Granny informed him.

She straightened her back, which had stiffened up, and walked past them—right into the ocean!

"Thanks for drawing my bath, Sidney," she said.

Sid rushed over to pull her out of the water. "Granny, grab my paw," he urged her.

But Granny was floating on her back with

a blissful expression. "No way!" she told Sid. "This is my first bath in decades!"

"Quick!" Sid looked helplessly at his friends. "Somebody do something!"

Manny did something. He threw Sid into the water to save her.

Sid snatched Granny and started to haul her in like a lifeguard. "I got you, Granny. Don't worry," he told her.

She slapped him. "Get off me!"

Sid finally managed to pull her back onto the iceberg, where Granny glared at Manny and Diego. "What are you two looking at? A lady can't take a bath in peace?" With that, she marched off.

Diego let out a big sigh. "What's the life expectancy for a female sloth?" he wanted to know.

"She'll outlive us all," Manny told him. "You know that, right? It's the spiteful ones who live the longest."

A short while later, Manny stared out at the vast ocean as the hot sun beat down on them. All he could see was water and some distant fog. "How big is this ocean?" He moaned in frustration.

They were all exhausted and hungry by now. And Sid was muttering to himself, "Water, water everywhere. Nor any drop to drink. Except for . . ." He raced across the iceberg and dipped his head into the ocean. His face puckered up as he lapped up some seawater.

"That's a little salty," mumbled Sid.

Abruptly, Granny got up. "Precious?" she said, looking around for her pet again. "Mommy is calling you. Precious? Come here, sweetie!" She almost stepped off the iceberg into the water again, but Manny yanked her back with his trunk.

"Hey, lady," she said to Diego. "Have you seen Precious?"

The saber-toothed tiger scowled. "If you mean the imaginary, or perhaps deceased, pet that you keep searching for, then no. I haven't seen Precious."

Squawk! Squawk!

A sound caught Manny's attention. "Look,

guys!" he exclaimed. "A bird! And where there are birds, there's land, right?"

Diego leaped up in excitement. "Hey, buddy," he called to the bird. It was a seabird with a cap of red feathers. "Come here!"

The bird eyed them . . . and then quickly flapped away.

"No!" shouted Manny. "Wait! Come back!"

But the bird kept going, disappearing into the foggy mist that lay ahead.

"It's a huge bounty, Captain Gutt," the bird, Silas, reported a few minutes later. He had landed on the shoulder of a mean-looking orangutan with a long beard. The orangutan stood at the bow of a pirate ship. "Four passengers—ripe for the taking," Silas went on.

"In my ocean?" the pirate captain snarled. "What a terrible turn of events." He paused and let out a sinister laugh. "I love a terrible turn of events!"

Diego blinked as he caught sight of something emerging from the fog ahead. "Am I hallucinating, or is that ice coming straight at us?" he asked.

Manny felt his spirits lifting. "Yeah, it's coming! And it sounds like there are some animals on it."

"Yippee!" Sid cheered. Then he started chanting. "We're being rescued! We're being rescued! We're being . . ."

"I hear . . ." Diego was still watching the iceberg uneasily. "Laughter."

"Oh!" Sid exclaimed happily. "It must be a party cruise."

Just then, two grappling hooks shot out from the approaching ship and grabbed hold of their iceberg, pulling it in.

"Yikes!" Sid said as their iceberg slammed into the other ship. Then he swallowed hard. Staring back at them was a fierce-looking crew—of pirates!

"Get ready to slice and dice, boys," a rabbit pirate said in a low voice.

"Knock it off, Squint," a white saber-toothed tiger named Shira snapped at him. "Wait for Captain's orders."

Just then, a voice rang out from above. "Ahoy, down there, mates!"

Manny and the others looked up. Another

pirate—a massive orangutan—was grinning down at them from the ship's rigging.

"How lucky are you?" the orangutan said with a chilling smile. He swung down onto the deck, landing near Manny with a loud thud. "You know, these waters aren't safe—they're infested with pirates. I'm glad we found you before they did. I'm Captain Gutt," the orangutan went on. "Here to help."

"That's a nice monkey," Granny piped up.

Manny gulped as the pirates gazed at them hungrily. "Look," he said, trying to reason with the pirate captain. "We don't want any trouble. We just need to get back to the continent."

"The continent?" Captain Gutt echoed. "That pile of rubble?" His crew members all laughed heartily.

Manny didn't understand what was so funny. "My family is there," he went on. "So if you could just—"

Captain Gutt's face instantly darkened. "Your family?" he spat back at Manny.

"That is *so* sweet. I hope you said good-bye to them because there's no way back to the continent!"

"Oh yes, there is!" another crew member blurted out. It was an elephant seal named Flynn. "Don't you remember, Captain? You can sail to Switchback Cove and catch the current back from there!" He tapped his head proudly and grinned. "This noggin is like a steel trap."

"See!" Manny said to his friends. "I knew there was a way home!"

"Thank you, Mr. Flynn," Captain Gutt said sarcastically. Then he stomped hard on the elephant seal's tail, instantly erasing Flynn's smile.

"There is no home!" Captain Gutt snarled at Manny. "There is only here! And here, your ship belongs to me. Battle stations!" he called to his crew.

With that, several panels slid open on the pirates' ship and a row of cannons pointed at Manny and his friends.

"Surrender your ship!" Captain Gutt

ordered. "Or face my fury!"

"Huh?" said Sid, confused. "Or face your furry what?"

"Not *furry*," Captain Gutt corrected him. "Fury." He barked out another command to his crew. "Fire!"

Manny ducked as several cannonballs made of ice shot toward him. Then the rabbit named Squint began firing off rounds of starfish. The sharp weapons embedded in his tusks.

"Ha-ha!" Squint laughed loudly, imitating a carnival worker. "Hit the mammoth, and win a prize!"

Diego, meanwhile, was trying to reach the vines that the pirates had used to join the two ships.

But Captain Gutt had noticed what Diego was doing. "Fire the starboard cannons!" he yelled.

Raz, the kangaroo, used her powerful feet to kick ice cannonballs at Diego.

"Fetch, Shira!" Captain Gutt ordered.

"Got him, Captain!" Shira answered. She leaped in front of Diego, cutting him off.

"Aw," she growled. "You almost made it."

"I don't fight girls," Diego snarled.

Shira suddenly grabbed a vine, whipping it in Diego's face. Swiftly, she knocked him down and pinned him.

"I can see why you don't fight girls," Shira replied.

The huge elephant seal had managed to pin Sid, too.

"Sid!" Manny cried when he saw his friend go down. But before Manny could go to Sid's rescue, Raz cut him off.

"Let's rumba, Tiny!" the kangaroo goaded Manny. Then Captain Gutt fired a huge ice ball, drilling Manny right between the eyes.

Manny wobbled for a second and then fell down, unconscious. The pirates let out a triumphant cheer.

"Lights out, big fella!" Captain Gutt laughed.

When Manny came to, he heard music. It was Flynn playing the accordion, he slowly realized. "Hello," the elephant seal greeted him.

Manny tried to move, but the pirates had tied him up. He suddenly felt a shadow. Looking up, he saw that Diego was tied up, too, and hanging overhead from a horizontal part of the rigging.

"Hey, buddy," Diego said. "Welcome to the party."

Captain Gutt dropped in front of Manny. "Morning, Sunshine. Let me be the first to extend the hand of friendship." He reached toward Manny.

"That's your foot," Manny muttered.

"Nothing gets by you!" Captain Gutt shot back.

"Where are we?" asked Manny. "What do you want?"

"I bet you're feeling lost, scared, confused?" Captain Gutt taunted him. "Allow me to explain. I'm a primate pirate pioneer, and these are my brave buccaneers, all of whom were once lost souls like you!"

"We owe our lives to Captain Gutt," Shira chimed in.

"And assuming he doesn't kill you," another crew member called, "you will owe Captain Gutt, too! He's the Master of the Seas!"

"Kill them? Me?" Captain Gutt laughed and looked at Manny. "No . . . at least not this very large and useful mammoth!"

Manny smirked. "Captain Gutt, really? I have a paunch belly, too, but I wouldn't name myself after it!"

"Ha-ha! That's funny!" Captain Gutt let out a loud laugh. "You're a funny guy. But that's not how I got my name." As Gutt held out his deadly claws, an icy shiver went through Manny, and Gutt's crew instantly stepped back. "These got me my name," Gutt went on.

Sid was staring at the pirate's claws, too. "I don't get it," he said.

"No?" Captain Gutt said. "Okay." He sliced the vines holding Sid so that Sid now hung upside down in front of him. "Let me show you." The pirate placed one of his sharp nails just below Sid's throat.

"I just gently press here and then move my paw down like this."

"Oh!" Sid giggled. "That tickles! Stop!"

Manny gulped as Captain Gutt pressed his claws into Sid's stomach.

"And soon your innards become your outards!" Squint chimed in. He let out a menacing laugh.

"Uh . . ." Sid looked confused. "I still don't get it," he mumbled.

"Look," Manny said to Captain Gutt. "As much as I'm tempted to join a monkey, the Easter bunny, and"—he looked at Flynn's huge and wrinkled body—"a giant bag of pudding, I'll pass. No one is going to stop me from getting back to my family."

"I'm going to lambada with your liver, buddy!" Squint cried, lunging at Manny with a knife.

Captain Gutt swiftly grabbed the rabbit and tossed him aside. Then he glared coldly at Manny. "That family is going to be the death of you." He spun back to his crew and barked out an order to his first mate, Shira.

"Jettison the dead weight!"

"Aye, aye, sir," Shira replied. "Prepare the plank!" she commanded Flynn.

"Prepare the plank!" the other pirates echoed.

Flynn pushed a plank halfway off the ship while the other pirates cheered. Then Raz grabbed Sid and hopped over to the plank with him.

"What?" Sid blinked in surprise. "You want me to walk into the water? I can't do that," he said. "Because I just ate, less than twenty minutes ago, and you know the rule about waiting before you go swimming."

Raz shook her head. "That's a myth," she informed Sid.

"Oh, okay then," Sid replied. "As long as it's safe."

"Wait!" Captain Gutt called out. He pointed at Granny. "Dump the wench, too."

A fierce-looking boar brought her over to the plank.

"Ladies first," Captain Gutt said, gesturing at the plank.

"He's such a nice boy," Granny said as she brushed past Sid. "Why can't you be more like him, Sidney?"

"Granny!" cried Sid. "No, wait!"

Manny struggled to break out of the vines. He couldn't get free, but his movements were shifting the boom arm where Diego was tied. Slowly, the arm inched closer to the vine that held the ship's mast in place.

Diego had noticed what was happening, too. "Manny! Get me to the vine!"

"Got it!" Manny signaled back. He was already wriggling harder.

Diego began wriggling, too, leaning hard toward the taut vine. Soon the vine holding the mast was just inches away.

"A little more!" he urged Manny.

Manny strained hard, rotating the mast slightly.

By now, Granny was at the end of the plank. A pack of hungry narwhals circled below. "Hey!" said Granny. "Y'all got some ugly goldfish!"

At last, Diego managed to extend his neck so that the tip of one of his sharp teeth touched the vine. Diego quickly sliced the vine, and with a *ping*, it snapped, unloosening the mast. The mast swung forward and was then pulled back by the vine on the other side.

Now Manny was able to stand up. Moving quickly, he grabbed hold of the mast and ripped it out of the ship.

"No!" Captain Gutt cried, looking up. He grabbed his sword and swung it at Manny.

Manny used his tusks to block the pirate's blows.

Gutt's crew cheered on the captain. "Yeah! Extinct that mammoth!" called Squint.

"Come on, Manny!" cried Sid. "Kick his monkey butt!"

"Look at you!" Captain Gutt jeered. "Eleven tons of land lubber blubber!"

"Hey, I'm not fat! I'm . . . uh . . . poofy!" Manny replied, offended. The two continued sparring and Manny blocked another swing of Gutt's sword.

"I could have used you!" the orangutan went on.

"It's not going to happen, Captain," Manny shot back. With that, he lunged at the mast, knocking it out of the ship.

Crack!

The pirates leaped backward as their ship began to buckle. Then a tree fell, smashing the deck and sending the pirates flying.

Sid dashed to Granny's rescue. "I got you, Granny!" he said.

She scrambled up his back, riding him like a horse. "Giddyup! Let's go!"

There was another violent crack as the pirates' ship split in two. As the two sections tilted upward, everything on the ship spilled into the sea.

"No!" bellowed Captain Gutt, clinging to the ruined iceberg.

Meanwhile Flynn thrashed about helplessly in the water. "They sank our battleship! What are we going to do? We're all going to drown!"

Captain Gutt reached out to grab the seal's snout. "Flynn! You're a *sea* creature, you idiot!"

"Oh. Good point, sir," the elephant seal replied.

Gupta, the badger pirate, was ready to surrender. "Should I fly the white flag, Captain?" He had already started climbing the pole.

"No!" roared Gutt. "I'm going to mount his skull on our next ship!"

"Wait," Flynn said, looking around and seeing no sign of the white saber-toothed tiger. "What about Shira?"

Captain Gutt yanked the elephant seal

closer. "What about her?" he snarled.

"Yeah," chimed in Squint spitefully. "What about her?"

"Anyone else want to play captain?" Gutt shot back. When no one said anything he slapped Flynn's side and motioned for him to start moving. "Come on, blubber brain," he ordered. "Swim!"

As Flynn obediently began swimming away, the other pirates clung to him and swam in his wake.

Manny and his friends drifted in the water on an iceberg about the size of a lifeboat. The pirates were out of sight when Manny heard a splash in the water. "Hey! Gutt! Flynn! Anyone there?" someone yelled.

It was Shira. The white saber-toothed

tiger was paddling in the water, desperately trying to keep her head above the waves.

Manny and Diego rushed to the edge of the iceberg. "Here!" Manny said, holding out a leg. "Grab hold!"

Shira's face clouded when she saw them. "No!" she snapped. "Go away! I'd rather drown."

Diego shrugged. "Whatever the lady wants." But as soon as Shira sputtered under another wave, Diego grabbed her and pulled her onto the ice.

Shira coughed and spat out some water. "I *said*, I don't need your help!"

"You're welcome," Diego retorted calmly. "So . . . ," he went on, "care to join our scurvy crew?"

Shira looked at Diego and the others with contempt. "Two sloths, a mammoth, and a saber," she said. "You guys are like the start of a bad joke."

"We saved you," Diego reminded her. "So that makes you the punch line, kitty."

Shira tackled him. "Don't call me kitty!" She snarled.

"Okay, I won't!" he agreed. Then suddenly he flipped her. "Kitty!"

Granny was watching them fight. "If they kiss," she muttered, "I'm going to puke."

Peaches moaned.

Ellie looked up from the winding coastal trail. It was sunset and she felt tired. Ahead she could see the land bridge silhouetted against the sky. The mammals had made some progress today for sure, but there was still a long way to go.

"Maybe we should rest for a few hours," Ellie told the group. Most of the animals collapsed right away, just as exhausted as Ellie.

But Peaches was too upset to sleep. Instead she hung upside down from a tree branch, wide-awake as she stared out at the water.

"I miss you, Dad," she murmured miserably.

Suddenly, Ethan was in front of her, a quizzical look on his face as he stared at Peaches hanging upside down. "Well, that's something you don't see every day," he said.

"I've never seen a mammoth sleep like that."

"Ethan!" Peaches quickly dropped onto the ground, landing clumsily on her face. "It helps me think!" she said, embarrassed. "It gets blood to the old noggin and . . ."

Ethan just laughed as Peaches babbled on. She knew she wasn't making any sense.

"Uh . . . okay," Ethan said. "That's a little weird."

In the distance they could hear rocks crashing and the earth rumbling.

"So how are you doing?" Ethan asked. "You know, with all this."

"Honestly," Peaches blurted out, "I'm a little scared. Okay, I'm a lot scared." She shook her head sadly. "Everything we knew is gone."

"Yeah," Ethan agreed. "I was pretty scared, too . . . I mean, not scared. But ya know, like concerned." He hesitated for a second. "Hey. Um, do you wanna walk with me tomorrow? Try and get our minds off all this stuff?"

Peaches stared at him in surprise. "You want to walk with *me*?"

"Well," Ethan replied, grinning, "you did almost flatten me this morning. So I figure it can't really get worse than that, right?"

Peaches grinned back. "Yeah."

"There's just one thing," Ethan said. He paused. "You might want to lose the molehog."

"Oh!" Peaches said, trying to cover her surprise. "Louis? Yeah, sure! Not a problem."

"Great. See you later," Ethan said.

Wow! That was amazing! Peaches thought as he walked away.

A minute later Ellie came over with Crash and Eddie. "Someone looks happy," Ellie said, looking at her daughter's dreamy expression.

Peaches sighed. "Ethan's great, isn't he?"

"I know you like him, baby," her mother replied. "But just . . . don't let anyone change who you are, okay?"

"I know," Peaches said.

With her tail, Ellie grabbed a limb in the tree with Crash and Eddie. "Are you coming up?" she asked Peaches.

"Um . . ." Peaches looked into the darkness. She could see Ethan in the distance, sleeping on the ground. "I think I'm going to sleep down here tonight."

"Oh. Okay," Ellie answered. "Good night, baby," she added softly.

"Good night, Mom," Peaches called. Then she looked out at the dark water again. "Good night, Dad," she whispered.

The next day Sid sat on the edge of the iceberg as it drifted along. He was trying to figure out something. "Granny, why didn't our family want us? What's wrong with us?" he asked.

Granny was busy trying to eat a huge clam. "They think we're screwups. Hey," she added, handing him the clam. "Chew this up a little for me—okay?"

Diego was looking around at their iceberg, which was melting fast in the hot sun. "We'll never make it home on this thing."

"Well, maybe you should have thought of that before you capsized our pirate ship, genius," Shira grumbled.

"I was trying to escape," Diego reminded her.

"Wimp," Shira shot back. The two of them kept bickering.

"Whiner!"

"Crybaby!"

"Land!" Manny shouted out suddenly.

"Yeah, land!" Diego echoed. Then he realized what Manny had said. "Wait . . . what did you say?"

"Land! Over there!" Manny pointed to an island that was visible over the waves. "Everyone, paddle!" he ordered. "Paddle!"

Soon they were all staggering onto the island. All Manny could think about was getting home. "We have to build a raft," he announced.

"Manny." Diego just looked at him, exhausted.

Sid was gazing at something in the distance. "Wow," he muttered. "Shira must really hate building rafts."

"What do you mean?" Manny asked. Then he turned to see Shira making a run for it.

"Go get her!" yelled Manny. "She can help us get back home!"

"Shira!" Diego took off after the white saber-toothed tiger, catching up to her as she reached the island's peak. "Gotcha!" he cried, tackling her. They fought as they rolled toward a precipice. Then Diego pinned her.

"Let go of me!" she snarled.

"Where do you think you're going?" Diego demanded. Before she could reply, he looked past her, over a steep bluff. Down below, there was a cove. He watched as huge ice chunks floated along two channels in the water, and then were pulled rapidly out to sea by the strong current.

"It's Switchback Cove!" Diego exclaimed, remembering what Flynn had said about the cove. "It's the way home!"

Suddenly, Diego caught sight of something else: dozens of hyrax laborers. The tiny little, guinea pig-like mammals scuttled around, building something while a large figure bellowed orders at them. Then the voice called out another order: "Raise the mizzenmast, Flynn! Come on! Put your blubber butt into it! I want this piece of ice seaworthy by sundown—I have a date with a mammoth!"

"Oh no!" Diego gasped, a chill traveling up his spine. It was Captain Gutt and he was building a new pirate ship!

Manny and Diego found a heavy rock and used it block off the opening of a tree. Then they imprisoned Shira inside.

"Is this how you treat all your guests?" she demanded. "Let me out of here."

"Sure," Diego said sarcastically. "We totally trust you not to tell Gutt we're here."

Back at Switchback Cove, Captain Gutt was still barking out orders at the hyrax. "You call this a ship, you miserable runts? This is nothing. I want a ship, not a floating trash heap! Faster, you worthless, wormy, sorry excuses for shark bait weevils!"

"What did he say?" Flynn murmured to Gupta.

Gupta shrugged, nervously keeping an eye on the captain. "I don't know."

Captain Gutt cracked his whip at the hyrax. "Now get this chunk of ice seaworthy by sundown, or I will keelhaul the lot of you!"

Diego had shown his friends the cove with the two channels that led out to the sea. "You're right, Diego," Manny said excitedly. "It's the way home!"

"Yeah," Sid chimed in. "Too bad we don't have a ship."

"Sure we do," Manny said, gesturing at

Captain Gutt's new ship, which was nearly finished. "It's right there."

"Well, that's a flawless plan," Shira muttered sarcastically. "You want to pirate a pirate ship from pirates?"

"It pains me to say this," Diego said. "But she has a point. It's a crazy idea."

"Yeah, well—" Manny started to argue, but Sid quickly hushed him.

"Guys! Shhh! The trees have ears!" he said, gesturing to dozens of little hyrax who were peeking out from behind trees, bushes, and rocks, watching them.

"Wait a minute . . ." Looking at the small creatures, Manny suddenly had an idea. "Maybe we can help one another!" He leaned down to talk to a few of the hyrax. "Hey, little fellas. Come on out."

The hyrax stayed where they were, too afraid to move.

"It's okay," Manny coaxed them gently. "We're not going to hurt you."

The shy creatures stepped a little closer.

"How about you and us against the pirates,

huh?" Manny went on. The hyrax stared at him blankly. Finally, Manny sighed. "You have no idea what I'm saying, do you?"

He tried another approach. "Uh . . . ship . . ." He pantomimed the words. "Me . . . want."

Shira scoffed at him. "Nice try, Jungle Jim."

"Go ahead, make fun," Manny snapped. "He got it."

Just then a hyrax named Fuzzy came forward and gave Manny a banana. "Thank you," said Manny.

"May I try?" Sid came over.

"Knock yourself out," Manny muttered.

"Okay, watch this!" Sid told his friends. "Ahem." He cleared his throat and then began warming up his vocal cords. "*Me me me me*. Six sloths sip broth. . . . Six sloths sip broth. . . ."

When Sid was finally ready, he crouched down. Then he crossed his arms and grabbed his shoulders. "*Wooga, wooga, wooga, wooga,*" he said, speaking what sounded like gibberish, tapping his shoulders at the same time.

Scrat loves his acorns! While chasing this one,
he finds himself stranded on an ice raft!

Manny and Ellie's daughter, Peaches, is all grown up.

Sometimes she doesn't understand when
Manny is looking out for her.

Diego looks out for her, too . . .

when he's not running into Sid's sloth family.

Sid loves his family, even if they are a bit crazy . . .

When an earthquake strikes, creating a large crack in the earth, Manny, Diego, and Sid find themselves floating out to sea on a large chunk of ice.

On the other side of the crack, Ellie and Peaches
try to find their way to Manny.

At the same time, Scrat has found himself
a desolate island and a new friend . . .

while our heroes try to find land.

Before long, Manny and his friends
run into another seafaring crew.

They don't seem to like Scrat very much, either.

Peaches hopes that she and her mom will find
her dad soon. She misses him a lot.

"Yarg!" he went on, imitating a pirate, and then making some other strange sounds.

To Manny's astonishment, the hyrax began to nod and cheer.

Diego looked at Manny. He couldn't believe the scene in front of him either. "That they understood?" he said.

Fuzzy emerged from a huddle of hyrax, ready for battle.

"Yep! They're in!" Sid announced.

"Great!" Manny declared. "We'll free your buddies, and then we can all escape the pirates."

Sid did a quick translation for his friends. Fuzzy nodded and turned back to Sid to give him a high five.

That night Diego approached Shira's prison with some water, startling her. "Easy, kitty," he said. "Here's some water. You need it." He slipped a coconut shell filled with water through the bars.

Shira shoved it back at him. "I don't need anything from you!" she snapped.

"Fine." Diego shrugged. "Die of thirst. That'll really show me." He pulled the water back out of the cage.

"Wait!" Shira abruptly changed her mind. "I'll take it. . . . Thank you," she added as he slid it back to her.

"You know," Diego said, watching her lap up the water, "you have a way of saying 'thank you' that makes it sound like 'drop dead.'"

"It's a gift," Shira replied. Diego turned to go. "You're pretty soft for a saber," she said softly.

He whirled around. "Excuse me, I am not soft, okay? I happen to be a remorseless assassin."

"Diego-poo!" a voice called out.

They both turned to see Sid coming toward them. "Look," the sloth said to Diego. "I made you another coral necklace." He turned to Shira and explained with a giggle, "Diego keeps losing them."

Humming happily, Sid left, and the two saber-toothed tigers were alone again.

"I think I'm starting to understand why you're not in a pack," Shira said.

"Listen," Diego shot back. "I chose to leave my pack, alright?"

"Congratulations, Warrior Princess," said Shira. "So did I."

"Really?" Diego was surprised to hear that. "I know how hard it is to walk away from everything you know," he added softly.

"Oh great." Shira rolled her eyes. "Are we going to start braiding each other's fur now?"

"Funny," muttered Diego. "Really funny. Can I tell you the difference between you and me?"

"Um . . ." Shira took a guess. "I wouldn't still be wearing that necklace?"

Diego had forgotten that he was still wearing the necklace from Sid. He ripped it off his neck. "No," he told Shira. "We both might have wanted to opt out of pack life, but at least I didn't trade one pack for another. I got something more."

"Oh yeah? What's that?" she asked.

"A herd," he replied.

"What's the difference?" Shira wanted to know.

"We're a family," Diego told her. "We have each other's backs."

"Gutt has my back," Shira retorted. "I'm his first mate."

"Not this time," Diego said. "I don't see Gutt sending out any search parties for you."

Shira didn't say anything for second. Then she spoke up. "You know you won't beat him. Your big furry friend over there . . ." She gestured toward Manny. "He has no idea what he's up against."

"Yeah," Diego admitted, looking over at his woolly mammoth friend, too. "But Gutt doesn't know what he's up against either."

The next day Manny brought everyone into a huddle. "Okay, let's review our plan. Fuzzy?" he said to their new hyrax friend. "You've got your end covered, right?"

Fuzzy did an elaborate kung fu routine in response.

"I'm going to take that as a yes," Manny said. "Diego? What about you?"

"I'll free Fuzzy's little friends."

"Sid and Granny?" asked Manny.

"Sir!" Sid snapped off a salute. "Untie the ship, sir!"

"Right, unwind the vines, and don't let go of them until we're all on board," Manny reminded him. "We're all relying on you, Sid. You got that?"

"Yes, sir, totally focused, sir!"

"Don't worry," said Granny. "It will be easy since we don't have to guard Shira anymore."

Everyone looked over at Shira's cage, which was empty now. Then Diego and Manny looked off in the distance, where they could see Shira racing toward the pirate camp.

"We need to move!" said Manny. "Now!"

Captain Gutt looked around his new pirate ship. "Batten down the hatches! Hoist the anchor and fly the colors! We're setting sail for vengeance, lads!"

"Captain!" Shira yelled. She raced toward them, panting.

"Shira! What a relief!" the pirate captain called. "I thought we'd lost you."

Shira eyed the captain doubtfully. He sounded concerned; did he really mean it? "The mammoth . . ." She panted, trying to catch her breath. "He washed ashore with me. He's—"

"He's here?" Captain Gutt cut her off, nearly drooling at the thought of Manny being so close by. "Did you sink your fangs in him?"

Shira looked away. "No. The saber took me down."

"What?" Captain Gutt bellowed in anger. "You're a failure!" He backed her up against a tree. "I need warriors! And all I have are kitty cats and bunny rabbits."

"And a seal and a kangaroo!" piped up Flynn helpfully.

Gutt closed his eyes in frustration. "You

take the saber down, or you die trying," he snarled at Shira. "Got that?" He pressed his claws under her chin. "No excuses!"

"Yes, Captain!" Shira promised.

The orangutan released her, smiling. Then he addressed the rabbit. "Mr. Squint, you're first mate now."

"Yo, ho, ho, and a bottle of cool with me, Captain!" Squint said in delight. Then he shoved Shira aside. "Out of my way, saber. You answer to me now."

"Gutt, listen," Shira started to explain. "He's coming to—"

Dooo-doot-do-dooo!

Before she could finish, a high-pitched battle call rang out. Over at the nearby hillside rows and rows of hyrax stood, armed with tiny lances, ready for battle.

Captain Gutt burst out laughing at the tiny soldiers. But a second later, his expression changed completely. Another battle call rang out, and this time Gutt spotted Manny behind the army of hyrax.

The pirate's eyes narrowed in anger. "Grab your weapons, mates!" he called to his crew. He looked at Flynn, who had picked up a spoon. "Not the spoon, Flynn! Follow me!"

"Oh yeah!" Squint said eagerly. "Let's do this!"

Captain Gutt bounded up the hill toward Manny, his crew right behind him.

In his hiding spot, Diego waited until Captain Gutt and the others rushed past. Then he raced over to the pens where Gutt had imprisoned the other hyrax, and knocked the locks off their cages. The grateful hyrax rushed over to Diego and hugged his legs.

"Guys, that's not necessary," Diego told them, embarrassed. "Really. I love you, too."

Meanwhile Sid and Granny were unmooring the ship's docking vines, one by one. Together they chanted, "Unwind the vines, don't let go. Unwind the vines, don't let go."

"Unwind the— Hey! What's that?" Sid

yelled, suddenly spotting a bush filled with purple berries. "Ooh!" he cried. "Yummo!"

Diego headed toward Sid, the hyrax from the cages still clinging to him. Diego panicked when he saw the berry in his friend's hand. "Sid! No!" he cried in alarm. "It's a lotus berry! It will paralyze you!"

"Oh, please," Sid scoffed. "I know my berries." He popped the purple berry into his mouth. "See. I'm fine. If there's one thing I know, *ith's behwees* . . ." Sid looked at Diego. His tongue was already beginning to swell and his body was going numb. A moment later he collapsed in a heap.

As Captain Gutt and his crew continued charging toward Manny, the hyrax soldiers held out their lances. Just before the pirates reached them, the hyrax used their lances to spring into the air. The tiny creatures landed neatly on the hyrax-driven leaf planes flying above in tight formation.

Squint's beady eyes were fixed on Manny. The rabbit pirate jumped onto a rock and then catapulted into the air, launching himself right at Manny's head. "Yeah! Finally!" Squint screamed in triumph.

Squint slammed into Manny's face—and the giant mammoth instantly collapsed!

Captain Gutt stared down at his feet where the mammoth's head lay. "No!" he bellowed as he realized what Manny and the others had done. The head at his feet wasn't the mammoth—Manny and the hyrax had made a decoy out of sticks and leaves!

Manny was already bolting across the beach toward the ship. "Move fast!" he cried to his friends. "He bought it!"

"Come on," Diego urged the freed hyrax as they all raced across the beach.

"No! No! No!" shouted Captain Gutt to his crew. "It's a diversion!"

"I know," Flynn said. "I'm having a blast!"

"No, pinhead!" Gutt swatted the seal in anger. "They're stealing my ship!" he cried. "Shira! Get the saber!"

With a roar Gutt raced after Manny. The other pirates followed him while Shira ran to intercept Diego.

Manny groaned when he reached Sid and saw him lying on the ground. "One thing, Sid," he muttered. "You couldn't do one thing?"

He poked the sloth, who didn't move. "Sid? Can you hear me? Say something, buddy!"

Still paralyzed from the lotus berries, Sid stared past Manny at something else. It was the last vine, the one holding the pirates' new ship to the dock. It was unwinding, and the boat was starting to drift toward the channel! Sid gulped, but he couldn't speak to warn his friends.

By now the pirates had almost reached them. "Let's go!" Diego said urgently.

Manny scooped up Sid and turned to the ship. Now he realized what was happening, too. "Come on!" he cried. "We have to catch the ship before it hits open water!"

Carrying Sid, Manny frantically raced after the ship. Diego and Granny followed, the band of pirates at their heels.

Silas suddenly dive-bombed into Manny. "Say adieu, mammoth!" the bird squawked.

"Ow!" Manny used Sid's limp body to slap the bird away. "Sorry, Sid!" he apologized.

At last, they neared the ship, and Manny managed to toss Sid aboard. But Sid slid right off the boat, landing on the ice below.

"I'm coming, Sid!" yelled Manny. He quickly knocked over a pillar of ice to make a bridge to get to Sid. But as the pillar struck the ice under Sid, the sloth flew high into the air.

"I've got you! I've got you!" Manny cried, standing below the sloth and bracing himself for the catch.

Meanwhile, on the shore, Captain Gutt blew a high-pitched whistle to summon a pod of narwhals.

Gutt jumped on the backs of two narwhals. "I'm coming for you, mammoth!" he yelled at Manny.

Manny stomped the ice beneath his feet, flipping part of it up to use as a shield. The narwhals slammed into the shield like darts. Their force sent Manny, Sid, and Granny sliding over an embankment and onto the ship.

A moment later Manny, Sid, and Granny were on board the pirate ship. As the current pulled it rapidly toward the open bay, Diego sprinted to catch up.

"Come on, Diego!" Manny urged his friend.

Diego was about to leap aboard when Shira tackled him. He looked right into her eyes. "Why are you doing this?" he demanded.

"You don't understand," Shira said. "I

don't have a choice!"

Diego shook his head. "You don't have to live this way, Shira!"

Shira stared at him, unsure of what to do.

"You'll be safe with us. We take care of each other," Diego told her.

Manny grabbed a tree onshore with his trunk, straining mightily to hold the ship in place for Diego.

"I can't hold on much longer!" Manny called to his friend. A second later, he lost his grip, and the ship shot forward again. "Diego!" Manny cried helplessly.

"Shira, come with us," Diego pleaded urgently. "Come with *me*!"

Shira nodded and the two of them took off, racing toward the ship. A second later Diego leaped aboard. But Shira hung back.

"Shira! What are you doing?" Diego cried.

"I've got your back," she told him. She threw her shoulder into a wall, knocking debris in the way of Captain Gutt just as he lunged toward the ship. The pirate fell to the ice below.

Diego stood helplessly on deck, watching her. By staying back, Shira had given them the precious seconds they needed to escape. But as his eyes locked with hers, Diego knew that Shira would pay dearly—probably with her life.

Manny gave Captain Gutt a triumphant salute while Granny waved at the furious orangutan.

"So long, Banana Breath!" she yelled. "Thanks for the ship!" All around Manny and his friends, the hyrax landed safely on ice floes of their own. Back onshore, Captain Gutt stormed over to a glacier. Roaring with effort, he broke off a massive piece of ice and slammed it into the water. "Shore leave is over!" he snapped at this crew. "Get your sorry carcasses on board now." The crew hurried aboard, then Gutt whistled for the narwhals to come and propel the iceberg out to sea.

Shira gulped as the pirate captain whirled toward her. "Gutt, I can explain," she began nervously. "He—"

But Captain Gutt didn't let her finish. Instead he pulled her in very close to him. "When this ends, I'll have a tiger skin hanging on my wall; I don't care whose. That mammoth has taken my ship, my bounty, and"—he eyed Shira—"the loyalty of my crew. I will destroy him and everything he loves," he vowed.

"**W**ait for it. . . . Wait for it!" said Crash. The possums were perched at the tops of two tall trees. They were watching a section of earth roll toward them, as if they were surfers and it was a giant wave.

"Woo-hoo!" the possums cried, riding the

wave of rock and debris. They landed hard on the ground but then popped up again, laughing.

"That was awesome!" cried Crash. He and Eddie hurried to catch up with Louis, who stared at them in wonder.

"Can I ask you guys something? Why are you both so happy? Don't you get it—the world might be ending?"

Crash looked at Eddie. "Can I tell him our secret?" he asked.

Eddie nodded and then Crash waved Louis closer so he could whisper in his ear: "We're very, very stupid."

This wasn't new information for Louis. "But still . . ." He prodded them. "Aren't you just a *little* concerned about dying?"

The two possums stared at him blankly. Then Crash reached out to touch Louis's nose. "Beep!" Crash said.

Louis just shook his head. He'd never understand the possums. "I'm going to find Peaches," he said.

* * *

At that moment Peaches was walking with Ethan and some other teenage mammoths.

"Hey, guys!" Ethan called, spotting a canyon that had just been formed by the shifting land. "Over here. Come on. It's a shortcut, and you're going to love it."

"Come on, girls," the mammoth named Steffie said to her friends. "Let's have some fun!"

Peaches followed the others into the narrow canyon. The sunlight bounced off the sandstone walls, creating an orange glow. The mammoths took turns calling out their names and then listening to their voices echo all around.

"Wow," Peaches said, looking around. "This is so cool! Echo!" She laughed when she heard her voice bounce back at her.

Steffie narrowed her eyes. "Too bad your molehog friend isn't here, huh?" she said suddenly to Peaches.

"You're not really friends with him, are you?" asked Ethan.

"Yeah!" Katie put in. "Come clean, Peaches."

Steffie leaned into Peaches's face. "Are you friends with that awkward little rodent or not?"

Peaches flushed. "I mean, Louis and I, we've hung out or whatever . . ." She could feel Ethan staring at her. "But no, we're not really friends," she blurted out.

"We're not friends?" a familiar voice echoed.

As Louis burrowed up from the canyon floor, Peaches felt the blood rush to her face. "Louis, I . . ." Her voice faltered. "I . . . It's—"

"Busted!" Steffie mocked her.

"Good to know," Louis said coldly to Peaches. Then he disappeared underground again.

"Louis, wait!" Peaches yelled. Just then Louis bumped into a rock.

"He even runs away like a loser!" one of the girls said.

Peaches tried to go after him, but Ethan stopped her. "Don't stress, Peaches," he said. "You're with *us* now."

"Yeah," said Katie. "Stress is so stressful."

"If you're going to stress about something, stress about your hair," Steffie added.

Peaches didn't say a word. She just stared at the spot where she'd last seen her best friend.

Inside the canyon, a shadow moved over Peaches and the others. The teenagers looked up—and saw that the enormous rock wall had crept closer. Now it was rising up over the canyon.

"Whoa . . . ," everyone murmured.

"Uh, guys!" Peaches was alarmed. "We should get out of here!"

"Are you kidding?" another mammoth said. "This is epic!"

Just then, the canyon began to buckle. Behind them, the walls were caving in!

"Go! Go! Go!" shouted Peaches.

A massive wave of debris and soot from the collapsing wall swept toward them. The teenagers bolted toward the opposite end of the canyon.

They'd barely made it out of the canyon when . . . *Whoosh!* A huge plume of debris shot out from where they'd just been standing. The spiraling cloud hung in the air over them, slowly clearing. In front of them lay a sheer drop to the ocean.

Ethan and the other mammoths burst into hysterical laughter.

"How sick was that?" said somebody.

"Yo, that was insane!" Ethan chimed in.

They all high-fived with their trunks while Peaches just stood there watching them.

"Hey, Peach! Loosen up! Have some fun!" Ethan coaxed her.

"Fun?" Peaches echoed. "You call that fun? I'm out of here."

"Come on," Steffie snapped at her. "Do you really want to go back to hanging with a weird molehog freak and give all this up?"

"I mean, it's bad enough that your family is half possum," Ethan added.

"Bad enough?" Peaches shot back. "There is nothing 'bad' about being part of my family. I like hanging by my tail. And if you geniuses are normal, the species is going to end up extinct!" With that, she stormed off.

"Uh, yeah?" Katie muttered after Peaches. "Well, your species is going to be extinct first."

"We're the same species, genius," Ethan snapped at her.

Manny was listening to water lap against the pirate boat as they sailed across the ocean. Overhead the stars were out, and the sky was clear. Luckily, Sid was no longer paralyzed. But he was making up for lost time by talking nonstop now.

"Hey!" he said. "I can wiggle my toes again. The important one—the little piggy who went to market. And I'm talking again," Sid went on. "I had so many things trapped inside me that I couldn't say! Like, hey, I'm not dead. And why does a hurricane have an eye, but not an ear . . . ?"

"I'll push him overboard," Granny muttered as Sid rambled on. "You guys say it was an accident."

"I'm in," Manny said. "How about you, Diego?" Glancing over at his friend, he realized that Diego was pacing back and forth, looking distressed.

"Relax, buddy," Manny said. "Captain Crazy and his floating petting zoo are history. Come on! We're finally heading home!"

"I don't know what's wrong with me," Diego fretted. "I can't eat. I can't sleep. Maybe I'm coming down with something."

Manny chuckled knowingly. "I know what you've got. The l-word."

Sid nodded. "Right. Leprosy."

"No, Sid," Manny corrected him. "It's

four letters. It starts with an 'l' and ends with an 'e.'"

"Ah," said Sid. "Diego has lice."

"No," Manny told him. "Diego, my friend, is in love."

Diego blinked at Manny. "You mean with the *pirate*?" he said. "No."

"Shira's gotten under your skin," said Sid. "Just admit it."

"A rugged saber like you . . . ," Manny began.

"And a more rugged saber like her!" Sid finished.

"No, no, no." Diego kept denying it. "You guys are dead wrong."

Manny and Sid looked at each other, and then burst out laughing as they high-fived.

"Denial is the clincher!" Manny declared. "You're in love, pussycat!" he told Diego.

Then Manny and Sid started singing together, *"Diego and Shira sitting in a tree . . . K-i-s-s-i-n-g . . ."*

"Real mature, guys," snarled Diego. "Real mature."

Later, while the others slept, Diego moved to the bow of the ship to look at the stars and think things over. It had been an intense few days. As he stared out at the dark horizon, he realized that the ship was drifting toward a patch of thick, mysterious fog. And soon he could hear a beautiful female voice singing. She was calling his name in a dreamy tone.

"*Diego . . . Diego . . . .*"

Peering into the mist, he spotted the silhouette of a saber-toothed tiger. "Shira?" he called back, confused.

"*I wanted to come with you,*" the voice said.

Is that really Shira? he thought. *What's going on?*

"She's beautiful," Sid said suddenly.

Ahead of them on a rock was a female sloth mermaid. She was beckoning Sid and calling his name. "*Sid. I adore a sloth who cares nothing about personal hygiene.*"

"That's me!" Sid replied.

Next Granny approached, rubbing her eyes sleepily. She could see a handsome, muscular sloth holding a trident. "*Granny!*

Come to me, Granny . . . ," he called.

The ship drew closer and closer to the fog and the mysterious singing voices. Sid, Diego, and Granny stood at the bow, completely entranced.

Soon the voices woke Manny, too. When he got up, he saw that the ship was moving steadily toward some dangerous-looking rocks.

"Guys!" he called. "Aren't you paying . . ."

"Manny?" called Ellie's voice. *"Are you there?"*

Manny stepped forward, a lump in his throat. "Ellie?"

"We're over here, Manny."

Manny squinted into the misty night. Dimly, he could see two mammoths on the rocks ahead. *"This way, Daddy!"* he heard Peaches's voice say. *"I really need you!"*

"I know, honey! Stay there! I'm coming!" He steered the boat closer to the rocks.

Ellie's voice floated through the fog again. *"You were right, Manny. You're always right."*

"No, no. Look, Ellie, I was—wait a minute!" he realized. "Ellie would never say that to me!"

Now Manny knew that something was wrong, and he snapped out of his trance. But Sid, Diego, and Granny were still under the spell, staring straight ahead, oblivious to what was going on.

"The voices aren't real," Manny told himself. "The voices must belong to sirens— mermaids known for luring sailors to their death!" He had to tune them out. Quickly, he stuffed bits of kelp and ice into his ears to block out the sirens' voices. Then he sang as loudly as he could.

Thump! The ship struck a rock.

Oh no, Manny thought. "Don't listen to the voices!" he yelled to the others. "They're monsters! They're going to destroy the ship!"

The mermaid-like figure in front of Diego looked and sounded like Shira.

"Come on, tiger," she said. *"Swim with me."*

Meanwhile Sid was leaning toward the sloth siren, ready to kiss her.

"No, Sid!" Manny cried. He grabbed the rudder, frantically trying to steer the ship away from the sirens. As the ship lurched,

Sid fell forward, still under the spell, falling onto Diego and kissing *him* on the lips instead.

"Why are we kissing?" asked Diego.

"Um . . . because cruises are romantic?" replied Sid.

As Manny finally turned the ship around, the sirens let out a furious wail. Manny heaved a sigh of relief. "Five more seconds, and we'd have been goners," he muttered.

Sid looked back over his shoulder. "Call me," he said to the sloth siren.

Granny was tossing fruit off the back of the ship and talking to the ocean. "Here, girl! Here, Precious."

"She thinks she finally found her pet," whispered Sid.

"Good girl," cooed Granny. "Here you go!"

Manny went over to her. "Look, Granny," he reminded her. "We don't have much food. Can you throw *imaginary* food to your imaginary pet?"

"Ignore them, Precious," muttered Granny. "I do."

"Oh man," Manny said, going back to his friends. "You can't take your eyes off her for one minute."

"It's like having a child," agreed Diego. "Only without any of the joy."

"Hey, Brain Trust! Brace for impact!" Granny hollered.

Manny quickly grabbed the rudder to steer them out of the way of dangerous pieces of debris. Suddenly, he realized that a familiar landscape loomed in front of them. "Guys!" he said excitedly. "We're almost home!"

Diego went over to him. "I never doubted you, buddy."

"Me either," piped up Sid. "Well, except for the six or seven times when I was sure we were going to die."

* * *

Ellie was at the front of the line of animals making their way to the land bridge. Peaches headed toward her, alone and looking distraught.

"What's wrong, sweetheart?" Ellie asked.

Peaches glanced at Louis, who was walking by himself, apart from the group. "Did you ever say something you knew you couldn't take back?" she asked.

Ellie glanced at the lonely looking molehog. "Is this about Louis?" she asked.

"I messed up so bad, Mom," Peaches blurted out.

"It's okay," Ellie said gently. "It happens. Cute boys can whiplash your brain. No doubt about that."

"But Ethan was the wrong guy," said Peaches.

"And you figured it out," Ellie reminded her. "You'll figure out what to say to Louis, too."

Peaches nodded gratefully. Just then she noticed that everyone had stopped walking. "What's going on?" she asked.

Ellie pushed her way to the front of the

line to see. "The land bridge!" she gasped. "It's gone. Oh no . . ." As Ellie stood there wondering what to do, she realized something else—the huge tower of rock was right in front of them!

"We're trapped!" one of the mammals yelled.

Peaches was in a panic. "But we were supposed to meet Dad here! What are we going to do?"

Looking around the water, Manny realized there was more debris—rocks and chunks of ice—scattered everywhere. In the distance, he could see the huge rock wall hanging over the bay. "Ellie! Peaches!" he shouted.

Diego gasped as he spotted something too. "Oh no! The land bridge!"

Sid gulped. "If it's gone, then how are we going to—"

"Sid!" Diego cut the sloth off before he could finish the ominous thought.

Manny felt a huge lump forming in his throat. *Ellie and Peaches survived*, he told himself. *Somehow, they survived.*

"They have to be on the other side," he told his friends firmly.

"Manny, there is no other side," said Diego softly.

"They have to be here," said Manny. And with that, he began calling their names. "Ellie! Peaches! I'm here!"

Diego and Sid exchanged worried looks. Manny didn't seem to understand what had happened. Nothing was left. The bridge—and their home—had collapsed and fallen into the sea.

Manny kept calling Ellie and Peaches. But only his own voice echoed back at him. His hopes began to falter. "Please . . . ," he murmured. "She has to be here. Then suddenly he looked at his friends. "Did you hear that?"

"No," they replied, shaking their heads.

"Manny," Diego began gently. "I think—"

"I heard something," Manny cut him off. He looked around, certain of himself. "I hear it!" Now, through the fog, he could see a silhouette moving toward them.

Diego saw it, too. "Is that—"

Manny's eyes brightened. "Peaches!" he yelled.

"Dad!" came a faint reply.

"We're coming, sweetie! Don't move!" Manny cried.

Manny grabbed the rudder and guided the ship toward his daughter.

"Daddy!"

"Peaches!"

As they drew closer, another shape emerged from the fog, and then a new voice rang out, "Welcome home, Daddy!" It was Captain Gutt, and he was holding a dagger over Peaches's head.

Manny was frozen with fear as he stared at the knife Captain Gutt held near Peaches. Now he could see that other mammals from home were tied up around the pirates' ship. Gutt had lured Manny and his friends into a trap!

"Let go of me!" Peaches cried.

Captain Gutt smirked at Manny as his crew moored the two ships together. "We were just talking about you!" the pirate declared. "What are the odds of meeting here like this?" Gutt gestured to the iceberg he was standing on. "Do you like my new ship? I call her *Sweet Revenge*."

Manny just shuddered in response.

"And look here," Silas chimed in. "We've got the catch du jour, the catch of the day." The bird gestured toward a mammoth tied up with vines.

"Ellie!" Manny called.

"I'm alright," Ellie called back. Then she glared at Captain Gutt. "Let my daughter go!"

"It's okay," Manny told Ellie. "He wants me. And he's going to get me!"

The pirates tossed their grappling hooks, pulling Manny's boat toward them. Diego snarled angrily and spotted Shira standing weakly off to the side. As she limped forward, he gulped. He could see that she'd been paying the price for their escape.

Captain Gutt grinned at Manny. "Sacrificing yourself for your daughter?" he said. "How touching. How predictable." He tightened his grip on Peaches. "Come and get her!"

Manny stopped in front of Gutt and Peaches. "Alright," he said. "Let them go."

"I don't think so," Gutt retorted. "You destroyed everything I had. I'm just returning the favor."

Abruptly Manny charged at the pirate captain. But Gutt's crew quickly lassoed him and tied him down.

"I warned you," said Captain Gutt.

"Stop!" a tiny voice yelled suddenly. Everyone whirled around as Crash and Eddie climbed aboard. But it wasn't the two possums who had spoken up, Manny quickly realized. It was . . .

"Louis?" said Manny in astonishment.

"Let the mammoth go!" Louis shouted at Captain Gutt.

"Uh-oh," Captain Gutt said, amused. "Who brought the muscle to the party?"

"Louis, don't do this!" yelled Peaches.

"What's he doing?" murmured Ethan. "He's going to get himself killed."

"It's okay," Louis replied. "I can handle him!"

"How cute," said Captain Gutt. "A hero. Let's see what bravery gets you." He turned to the badger pirate. "Gupta, give the lad your weapon," he ordered.

"Nice knowing you, kid," Gupta said, tossing Louis a knife.

The knife fell, embedding in the ice near Louis. He tried to grab it, but he wasn't strong enough. At last, he managed to grip the handle and yank it out.

Bravely, Louis faced the pirate captain. Gutt held one of Peaches's tusks while his other paw twitched at his side.

"Let's dance, hero," growled Captain Gutt.

To everyone's surprise, Louis tossed his knife high into the sky. It twirled in the air for a second before coming back down. By the time the knife landed in the ice, Louis had burrowed into the ground.

Confused, Gutt looked around. Then Louis

suddenly popped up near Gutt's feet. Louis swiftly grabbed a block of ice and plunged it into the orangutan's foot!

As Captain Gutt howled in pain, Peaches and Louis raced away from him.

"Run, Peaches!" cried Ellie.

"Get to the other ship!" Manny yelled to Peaches and Louis. He burst free of his vines.

"Don't stand there like barnacles! Get him!" Gutt called furiously to his crew. He made a move for Manny himself, but Diego stepped in his path.

"Not so fast, sea monkey." The saber-toothed tiger snarled. He lunged for Gutt and the two of them began battling furiously.

Sid and Granny swung across to the pirates' ship. They slammed into Flynn's belly, getting bounced to the ground. When the sloths got up, Gupta and Flynn chased them to the ship's edge.

"Any last words?" growled Gupta as he pointed his sword at them.

"Precious!" Granny cried.

"Would you stop with the 'Precious'?" Sid muttered to her.

Just then, a huge shadow rose over them. Sid saw the pirates' faces change to a look of terror.

"Well, I guess we showed them, huh?" said Sid.

"Precious!" Granny cried again.

Slowly, Sid turned around. Now he could see why the pirates looked so terrified. Behind them, an enormous whale had breached the surface, its mouth gaping open. Sid was stunned. "That's your pet, Granny?" he managed to say. "Wow, maybe that crazy old bat isn't that crazy after all!"

To his astonishment, Granny walked right inside the whale's open mouth! "Nope, she's nuts," Sid decided.

"Are you waiting for a formal invitation, fancy pants? Get in!" Granny snapped.

Sid hesitated one last moment. "I'm going to regret this," he muttered. Then he waddled inside Precious after Granny. The giant whale closed her mouth and then dived deep into the water.

Sid slid down the whale's throat.

"Ech," murmured Sid. "This smells worse than me." The whale's belly was filled with slimy, half-digested food.

"Precious!" Granny commanded. The muscles inside the whale instantly tightened as if Precious was snapping to attention. Granny went on. "Set your flippers forty-five degrees north. Granny's done running!"

Shira raced toward Ellie, who was still tied up on deck.

"Back off!" Ellie snapped at the saber-toothed tiger.

"It's okay. I'm on your side," Shira told her. As she slashed one of the vines binding Ellie, a Chinese star sliced past her face.

Shira whirled around to see who'd fired it.

"I knew you were a traitor," snarled Squint.

Shira glared at him. "Aw, your little bunny nose wiggles in the cutest way when you're mad."

"Your nine lives are over, kitty," Squint shot back.

A foot suddenly stomped the rabbit into the ice. It was Ellie. "Silly rabbit," she said. "Piracy doesn't pay!"

"Hey, that's not cool," whimpered Squint. "Come on now."

Before Shira could finish freeing Ellie,

Dobson rushed over and knocked the saber out of the way.

Seconds later, Precious breached the surface again near the ships. Sid popped through the whale's blowhole, covered in slimy stomach goop. "Yuck," he murmured, looking at himself. "Anyone have a body wipe?"

He stood on Granny's shoulders as she spun him around like a periscope.

"Suck it up, buttercup," she said. "How's it looking?"

"Not good, Granny, sir," Sid replied. On deck Raz, Silas, and Flynn were going after Manny while Gupta, Dobson, and Gutt had cornered Shira and Diego.

"Fire!" shouted Granny. Water shot from Precious's blowhole. Sid struggled to hold on as water sprayed violently, knocking Raz off her feet. As he swiveled, Sid suddenly realized that he could control the direction of the spray. He shot a water cannon at Dobson, and then fired off twin geysers at Gupta and Silas. Next was Flynn. Aiming carefully at the elephant seal's chest, Sid blasted Flynn right off the ship. Only Gutt managed to dodge the water cannons.

Manny blinked in surprise when he saw Sid sticking up from Precious's blowhole. "Sid?"

"Hi, Manny!" Sid waved.

Just then Precious slammed into the water, sending up a curtain of spray. As the spray cleared, a voice rang out. It was Ellie. "Help!" she called. She was still tied to the ship, and Gutt was moving toward her.

"Mom!" cried Peaches.

Manny ran in front of his daughter. "No, Peaches, stay right there!" Manny yelled. "I'll get her!"

With a smirk, Captain Gutt knocked away the log that connected the two ships, cutting off Manny's path. Then he held up his sharp claws. "Payback time!"

"Hurry, Manny!" cried Ellie.

Manny rushed desperately to the edge of the ship. But he was trapped, with no way to reach Ellie.

Peaches was watching in horror. Thinking fast, she launched herself at the rigging overhead. Then, as if she were back in the valley swinging from tree to tree, she used her tail to swing from mast to mast, moving across the ship toward Ellie.

"I got this, Dad!" Peaches declared.

"Peaches, no!" Manny said fearfully. "It's too dangerous!"

In one fluid motion Peaches swung off the last mast with her trunk extended.

Boom! She delivered a crushing punch to Gutt, knocking him off his feet.

"Wow! She did it!" Manny exclaimed in awe. He knocked down a mast to make a bridge while Peaches freed her mother.

"That's my girl!" Ellie said proudly.

"Ellie!" Manny yelled, rushing to his family.

Massive rocks fell from an overhang above, and then they heard a loud creaking sound. "We've got to get out of here!" Ellie cried.

"Go!" shouted Manny. "I'm right behind you!"

Ellie and Peaches leaped across to the other iceberg. But Captain Gutt cut off

Manny. "You're not going anywhere!" the pirate growled.

There was a tremendous splitting sound, and then the wall of rock crashed into the sea. The massive force split the iceberg, separating Manny and Gutt from the rest of the group.

"Look out!" yelled Peaches.

Captain Gutt quickly grabbed Manny's tusks, holding him tightly so he couldn't get away. Beneath them the ocean water rose, lifting the iceberg toward the sky.

The two animals continued battling fiercely with swords and bone weapons as their iceberg crashed down and then slid toward some perilous rocks.

"There's nowhere to run," yelled Gutt. "It's sink or swim, Manny! You know this ocean isn't big enough for both of us." He swung at Manny—and missed.

"Yeah, don't worry. You won't take up much space when I flatten you," cried Manny. He knocked Gutt back. But Gutt recovered quickly, using tree limbs to swing him forward.

Gutt kicked Manny backward. "Playtime

is over, mammoth. Told you, Tubby . . . you shouldn't have messed with the Master of the Seas!"

"Tubby? I've heard that one too many times."

Gutt stepped forward, holding up his gleaming claws. He jumped as the ice floor tilted, timing it perfectly so that his feet catapulted the pirate high into the air. Gutt shot toward Manny, and then Manny swatted him hard with his massive trunk. Gutt flew into the air, disappearing in the distance near a jumble of rocks.

Manny looked down. "Sometimes it pays to weigh eleven tons! Bon voyage, Monkey-boy!"

Manny was about to celebrate—until he realized that he was sliding full speed toward some deadly debris! Unable to stop himself, he slammed into an icy curve and went airborne. In the nick of time Precious leaped from the water, catching Manny in her open mouth.

"Did somebody hail a whale?" a familiar voice asked.

It was Sid, looking out from Precious's blowhole. "Mission accomplished, Granny!" he said.

"Ha!" Granny replied. "Who says old ladies can't drive!"

Far away, Captain Gutt surfaced from the ocean depths. Beautiful music filled the air.

"Captain Gutt," a female voice sang, luring him closer. "Let's rule the seas together . . ."

"Aye, aye," Captain Gutt answered in a dazed voice as he swam toward the sirens.

All Peaches and Ellie could see was water spraying everything. They moved to the edge of the iceberg to try to locate Manny in the sea. A second later they saw him—riding triumphantly on Precious's back!

"Dad!" yelled Peaches.

At the sight of Manny, all the teen mammoths cheered and high-fived with their trunks. The rest of the animals joined in the celebration, too, as Precious carried Manny over to his family.

"Manny!" cried Ellie.

"Dad!" cried Peaches, running to him.

Ellie turned to her daughter. "I told you your father would never give up on us."

"Never!" Manny confirmed. Just then Precious spouted, ejecting Sid and Granny. Manny went over to them. "You know, Sid," he told his friend, "you're not such a screwup."

"Aw, really?" Sid replied.

Manny grinned. "Really," he said. "You're a hero."

"You too, Granny," Diego chimed in.

"Thanks, lady," said Granny with a smile.

Shira was watching Diego. "Still want me on your scurvy crew?"

Diego grinned. "You bet," he replied. "Welcome to our herd." As Shira smiled back, Diego stepped closer to her.

Just then Peaches noticed Louis. "Hey, you, I can't believe you did that for me. Thank you."

"Well, someone once told me, no matter what, you never leave a friend behind," he replied.

Granny rolled her eyes. "All this sweetness would rot my teeth. If I had any," she added.

Later the mammoth family stood with Sid and Granny at the front of the ship, gazing at what was left of the coast.

"Our home is gone," Peaches murmured sadly. "Where do we go now?"

It didn't take long for the group to figure out an answer to Peaches's question.

Soon, Precious was powering the boat across the ocean.

Manny, Ellie, and Peaches gazed out at the water while Shira rested her head on Diego's shoulder. Diego smiled contentedly as Precious brought them closer to the New World—and to the hyrax's new home.

Tall trees and colorful flowers dotted the lush green landscape. Snowcapped mountains rose over the land in the distance. Overhead were flocks of chattering birds—along with dozens of hyrax, who were flying out in their tiny leaf-glider planes to welcome the newcomers.

As they landed, the hyrax named Fuzzy raced over to Sid, and the two friends quickly did their fancy dance ritual again. Meanwhile, a bunch of other hyrax surrounded Diego to give him a group hug.

"I love you, too," Diego said, grinning.

Shira was watching him with a smirk. "You're a remorseless assassin, huh?" she teased him.

"And don't you forget it!" he told her, grinning back.

Peaches and Louis were staring ahead, amazed by the hyrax's lovely home.

"I can't wait to check out this place," said Louis.

"Yeah!" said Peaches.

"Excuse me!" Manny said sternly.

"Dad!"

"When you two get off this ship, I expect you to—" He stopped as Peaches made a face. "Have fun," Manny finished.

"Huh?" said Louis.

"You're a brave kid," Manny told Louis.

"Wait, what?" said Peaches.

"You heard me. You two should go out and explore. Go where the day takes you," Manny went on. As Peaches beamed, he added, "But be back before sunset."

"An hour *after* sunset?" Peaches pleaded.

Manny pretended to look stern for a second. "Okay," he agreed. "But not a moment later!"

"Deal!" Peaches replied. "I love you, Dad," she added with a smile.

"Hey!" Ethan called to Louis and Peaches. "Is it okay if we hang with you guys?" He gave Louis a fist bump with his trunk.

"I always liked him, Louis the hero," said Steffie.

Manny and Ellie were watching Peaches among the teenagers. "She's not my little girl anymore," Manny murmured.

"And you're both going to be fine," Ellie said.

He smiled as she leaned her head on his shoulder. "Yeah."

Granny watched everyone exploring their new home. "You know, Sidney? You've got yourself a real nice family here," Granny said. "It's a *real* family."

"Yeah." Sid nodded. "I'm pretty lucky."

"Here." Granny handed him some fruit. "Chew this kiwi for me."

"Uh-uh." Sid shook his head. "Never again," he told her. Smiling, he handed her something. "Ta-da!" It was a set of fish teeth.

Granny popped the teeth into her mouth.

They look a little funny, Sid thought, *but they fit well enough.* Just like two sloths in a certain herd.